We Keep a Store

A RICHARD JACKSON BOOK

We Keep a Store

by **ANNE SHELBY**

paintings by **JOHN WARD**

ORCHARD BOOKS · NEW YORK

Orchard Books, A division of Franklin Watts, Inc., 387 Park Avenue South, New York, NY 10016

Manufactured in the United States of America. Printed by General Offset Company, Inc. Bound by
Horowitz/Rae. Book design by Mina Greenstein. The text of this book is set in 17 pt. ITC Esprit
Medium. The illustrations are acrylic paintings on paper.

10 9 8 7 6 5 4 3 2 1

Library of Congress Cataloging-in-Publication Data
Shelby, Anne. We keep a store / by Anne Shelby ; illustrated by John Ward.   p.   cm.
Summary: A small girl describes the many pleasures that accompany running a country store.
ISBN 0-531-05856-5.   ISBN 0-531-08456-6 (lib. bdg.)   [1. Stores, Retail—Fiction.   2. Country
life—Fiction.]   I. Ward, John (John Clarence), ill.   II. Title.   PZ7.S54125We   1989   [E]—dc20
89-35105   CIP   AC

To Uncle
who keeps a store
A.S.

To my family
J.W.

We keep a store.

It sits right in our front yard,
so whenever we need anything
all we have to do
is walk across the yard to the store and get it.

We don't even have
to pay ourselves for it.
That's one good thing about
keeping a store.

In a corner
behind the counter
there's a cardboard box.
When a customer wants candy,
my mother scoops a scoop into the box
and comes up with gum drops,
lemon drops,
and creams.

She slides the candy
into a paper sack
and weighs it on the big white scale.
Sometimes she has to take a little out
or put a few more pieces in.

When she isn't looking
I can eat a piece of candy
right out of that box.
That's another good thing about keeping a store.

My mother figures out
what to order from the big
grocery company.

When the truck comes, my father
slits the boxes open with his knife.
I help stack cans on shelves.

We all wait on customers
and put money in the cash register
and count out change.

We work together.
That's another good thing about keeping a store.

But our customers
don't come just to buy things.
They come to visit, too.

In winter, the men
circle their chairs around the stove
and tell long stories
about the old days
when wolves and bears and foxes roamed the country.

Sometimes they tease me.
"You ought to get married," they say.
"Leroy here would make you a good husband."
Leroy stares at his shoes.
My face turns red-hot, like the coals in that stove.

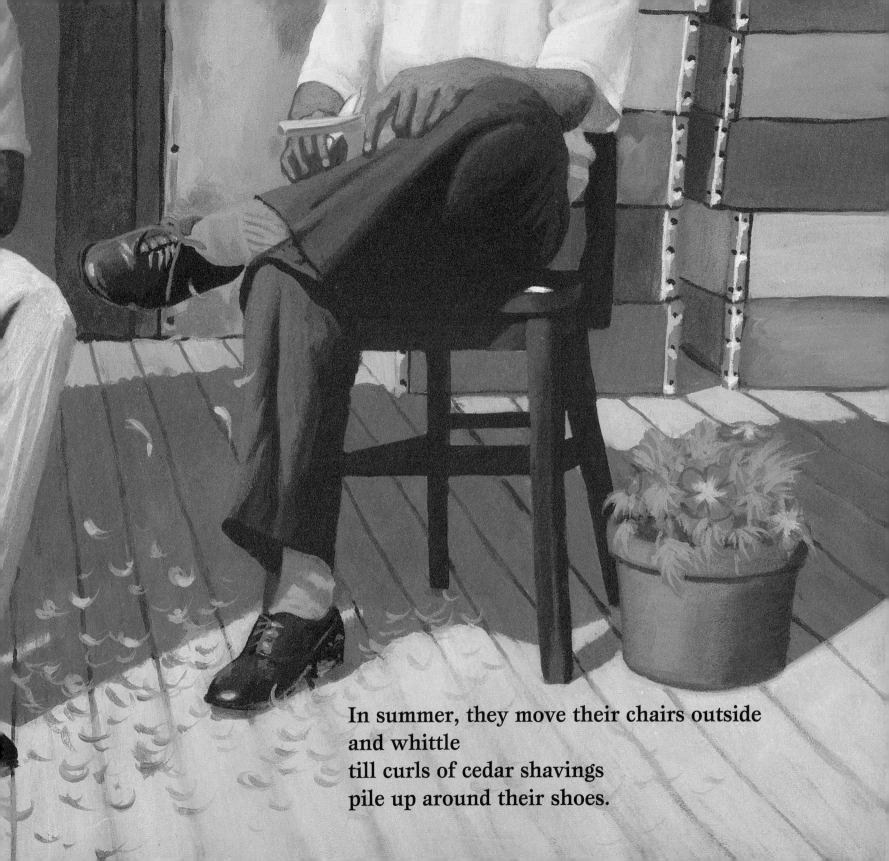

In summer, they move their chairs outside
and whittle
till curls of cedar shavings
pile up around their shoes.

The women sit with my mother
under the apple trees in the yard.
They help her string green beans to can
or cut apples up to dry.

Their children play with me
in the field beside the store.
We play kick-the-can
or hide-and-go-seek
or something we just make up,
like chase-that-chicken or
see-who's-the-first-to-fall-into-the-creek.

Finally, toward dark,
a grown-up hollers
for the children to come on, it's time
to go home.

"You all come back," my father tells them.
And they answer, "We'll be back."

They mean it, too.
That's the best thing about keeping a store.